ME and my DOG

written by
Michael Dahl

art by
Zoe Persico

Curious Fox
a capstone company-publishers for children

First published in 2016 by Curious Fox,
an imprint of Capstone Global Library Limited,
264 Banbury Road, Oxford, OX2 7DY
Registered company number: 6695582

www.curious-fox.com

Printed and bound in China.

ISBN: 978-1-78202-521-4
20 19 18 17 16
10 9 8 7 6 5 4 3 2 1

A CIP catalogue for this book is available from the British
Library.

This is me . . .

. . . and my dog.

My dog and I like to do
everything together.

Well, almost everything.

We love to play outside.

I like to swing, but my dog
doesn't want to swing.

He just wants to dig.

I love being loud and
crazy and adventurous.

SPLASH!

My dog likes being crazy
and adventurous, but he
HATES loud noises —

especially when he's sleeping!

I like sharing my toys.

But my dog doesn't always
like sharing his toys.

My dog and I both LOVE snacks.

But I can't share some
of my favorite snacks.
(Sorry, boy!)

NOT FOR DOGS!

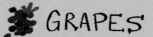 CHOCOLATE

GRAPES

CANDY

ONIONS

COFFEE

But no matter what
we do, my dog and I love
to be together best of all.

A NOTE FROM DOG

Hi friend,

    I like you and hope we can be friends forever. Here are a few things to remember to keep our friendship going:

- **BE KIND**: Pet your dog softly.
- **BE CONSIDERATE**: Do not chase or sneak up on your dog.
- **BE POLITE**: Let a sleeping dog sleep and an eating dog eat.
- **BE CALM**: Do not steal your dog's toys or play rough.
- **BE GENTLE**: Never hit, pull, poke, ride or tease your dog.
- **BE RESPECTFUL**: Respect your dog's space.

    Above all, treat your dog how you want to be treated. Your dog will be the best friend it can be if you're a good friend too!

Yours,

Dog